THE CENTER FOR CARTOON STUDIES PRESENTS

SATCHEL PAIGE

x x x STRIKING OUT JIM CROW x x x

James Sturm & Rich Tommaso
with an introduction by GERALD EARLY

Ðisney JUMP AT THE SUN

LOS ANGELES   NEW YORK

First Hardcover Edition, December 2007
Second Hardcover Edition, April 2019
First Paperback Edition, April 2019
10 9 8 7 6 5 4 3 2 1
FAC-029191-19067
Printed in Malaysia

Comic hand lettered
Remaining text set in Adobe Caslon Pro/Fontspring, Erased Typewriter 2/Fontspring
Designed by Jacob Covey, James Sturm, and Michael Vrána

Library of Congress Control Number for Hardcover: 2007061362
Hardcover ISBN 978-1-368-02232-3
Paperback ISBN 978-1-368-04289-5
Reinforced binding
Visit www.DisneyBooks.com

The Center for Cartoon Studies
P.O. Box 125
White River Junction, Vermont 05001
Visit www.cartoonstudies.org

Introduction

by Gerald Early

He stood six foot three and one-half inches. Lanky, with big hands and big feet. He would walk across the field to the pitcher's mound in the middle of a game knowing everyone had come to see him, was waiting for him. He would sometimes do "shadow" tricks with the ball while warming up, joke around, act as if he wasn't very serious about playing the game. But he was serious indeed when he began his windup to throw the first pitch.

When he played, he took no prisoners. He was the master of his pitches and the master of the head game of keeping batters off balance. For underneath his playfulness was a fierce, proud competitor. He was the prince of pitchers, the smiling, smirking god of black baseball. He was the most popular black baseball player in the country from the 1920s to the 1940s. He was the most photographed of all Negro League players and the highest paid. His name was Leroy Paige.

His nickname was "Satchel" because as a child he had worked hustling luggage at a train station. Satchel was a fitting name, for he spent most of his adult life traveling around the United States and the Caribbean, playing baseball. "Have glove, will travel" could have been his motto. "I'll pitch until I die" could have been another one, as he pitched professionally until he was in his mid-sixties.

Once upon a time in the United States, African Americans could not play on baseball teams with whites. The two races were segregated by law and by custom for nearly seventy years. During this time, African Americans had to endure insult, inferior treatment, and harsh conditions, even violence, from whites. But in the legendary days of the national pastime, blacks loved baseball as much as whites did, and since they could not play with whites, they formed their own teams. They even formed their own professional leagues.

Black baseball developed a thrilling style and became its own world. It was a fast-paced game of stolen bases, bunts, line drives, and clever base-running. The players made more money than the average black person at that time, often a lot more. But black baseball was no easy game to play; not only was it competitive, but the conditions were tough. Black ballplayers barnstormed relentlessly, going anywhere to play any professional or semiprofessional team. This made it tough for the leagues to succeed, because the teams could make more money playing nonleague games. Sometimes black teams would play three games in a day.

Umpiring was often not the best. The condition of the fields left much to be desired. Crowds were frequently rowdy, and travel was hard because of segregation. Blacks could not use public restrooms, eat at most restaurants, or stay at virtually any

hotel not in a black neighborhood. They had to ride from city to city on broken-down buses, not on trains, as white major league teams did. But these men loved the game and played it with great passion and skill. It was in this world and among these men that Satchel Paige lived his life.

Satchel Paige was born on July 7, 1905(?) in Mobile, Alabama. No one is sure of this date because Paige never told the truth about his age, and at the time the South did not keep very accurate birth records for African Americans. He was born into a poor family of twelve. Always pitching rocks at squirrels and rabbits to get extra meat for the family dinner table, Paige started pitching baseballs in school when he was ten. He began to pitch as a professional in 1924 and made it his life's work. He was sensational as a young pitcher, with a blazing fastball and wicked curve, so remarkable that as the years went by he became famous beyond just Negro League fans. He became so famous that people came just to see him pitch. Paige, realizing he was a star attraction, soon began to jump around from team to team

He was sensational as a young pitcher, with a blazing fastball and wicked curve, so remarkable that as the years went by he became famous beyond just Negro League fans. He became so famous that people came just to see him pitch.

to increase his salary. Sometimes he would pitch for several teams in the same year.

The Negro Leagues found it hard to stop their star players from doing that, and Paige did it more than anyone. The two teams that Paige became most associated with were the Pittsburgh Crawfords and the Kansas City Monarchs.

Jackie Robinson became the first black to play for the major leagues when he started for the Brooklyn Dodgers in 1947. In 1948, Satchel signed with the Cleveland Indians. He was forty-two, an age at which most players would have already retired.

The graphic novel you hold in your hands tells a bit of the story of Satchel Paige and the men of the Negro Leagues. It tells the story of what this game meant to the men who played it and to the people who watched it. For many of the black men who played, baseball was the great American Dream made real. Satchel Paige was one of those men, a great athlete and pioneer, who helped to make the ballparks of America level playing fields for everyone.

—G.E.

SATCHEL PAIGE

1929 AIN'T EASY LEAVIN' YOUR WIFE AND CHILD, BUT YOU CAN'T BE A BALLPLAYER UNLESS YOU WILLIN' TO TRAVEL.

FRANCES DON'T LIKE MY LEAVIN', BUT SHE'S AGREE-ABLE TO IT. SHE KNOWS WHEN I GET BACK, MY POCKETS WILL BE FULL. SHE CAN SPEND ALL HER TIME RAISIN' OUR BABY AND NOT SOME WHITE MAN'S KIDS.

I'M 18 YEARS OLD, AND I'LL BE MAKIN' MORE MONEY THAN HER DADDY AND MY DADDY PUT TOGETHER. AIN'T BRAGGIN' IF IT'S TRUE.

INSTEAD OF BRINGIN' HOME FORTY CENTS A DAY WORKIN' MR. JENNINGS'S FIELDS, I'LL BE MAKIN' SEVENTEEN DOLLARS A WEEK. MR. JENNINGS SURE MAKES THAT KIND OF MONEY BUT NO NEGRO THAT I KNOW.

TUCKWILLA, ALABAMA, IS COTTON COUNTRY. SHARE-CROPPER SHACKS EVERY WHICH WAY YOU LOOK.

NO SPECIAL CARE AS TO HOW THEY WAS BUILT 'CAUSE THEY WAS BUILT FOR NEGROES.

MAKE ME SOME MONEY, AND I'LL BUILD ME A REAL HOUSE FOR MY FAMILY. THEM SHACKS IS GETTIN' TOO SMALL FOR ME.

I ARRIVE IN MEMPHIS FIRST THING IN THE MORNIN' AND PLAY A DOUBLEHEADER THAT DAY AGAINST THE ST. LOUIS STARS. OVER THE NEXT TWO WEEKS, WE PLAY GAMES IN MONTGOMERY, TUSCALOOSA, AND SELMA. THE RED SOX LOSE PLENTY MORE THAN THEY WIN, BUT NOT ON ACCOUNT OF ME. I MAY BE THE YOUNGEST PLAYER ON THE TEAM, BUT NOBODY HITS THE BALL ANY BETTER.

TODAY WE TRAVELIN' TO PLAY THE BIRMINGHAM BLACK BARONS. SATCHEL PAIGE WILL BE PITCHIN'.

PAIGE AIN'T BUT A FEW YEARS OLDER THAN ME AND HE GETTIN' HIS NAME READ IN THE **CHICAGO DEFENDER** AND THE **PITTSBURGH COURIER**. YOU GET IN THE PAPERS, AND YOU MAKE A NAME FOR YOURSELF.

PEOPLE SAY HE'S THE NEXT BULLET ROGAN. LOOKS LIKE ROGAN, HARD THROWER LIKE ROGAN.

BIG CROWD AT RICKWOOD FIELD. BIGGEST CROWD I EVER PLAYED BEFORE. HOPE THERE ARE SOME NEWSPAPERMEN IN ATTENDANCE. I AIM TO SHOW EVERYONE I'M THE BEST, AND THE ONLY WAY TO GO ABOUT THAT IS TO BEAT THE BEST. MORE PEOPLE THAT SEE THAT, THE BETTER.

PAIGE'S CATCHER, BILL PERKINS, IS BUCKLIN' UP, BUT NO SIGN OF PAIGE.

NEARIN' GAME TIME AND THE PITCHER'S MOUND STILL EMPTY.

UMPIRE HEADS OVER TO THE BARONS' DUGOUT AND HAS A WORD WITH THE MANAGER.

UMPIRE YELLS, "PLAY BALL," AND LIKE EVERYONE ELSE IN THE PARK, I'M LOOKIN' FOR PAIGE.

THEN I SEE HIM, TALL AND LANKY, SHUFFLIN' ACROSS THE INFIELD. HARD TO BELIEVE THAT A MAN WHO MOVES SO SLOW CAN PITCH SO FAST.

PAIGE TAKES A FEW MINUTES ADJUSTIN' THE LACES IN HIS RIGHT SHOE.

NEXT, HIS SHIRT GETS TUCKED IN AND BELT BUCKLE TIGHTENED.

OUR LEADOFF HITTER, CONNIE WESLEY, STEPS INTO THE BATTER'S BOX. PERKINS STILL AIN'T TAKIN' HIS CROUCH.

NOW THE LEFT SHOELACE.

THEN A FEW MINUTES WORKIN' THE DIRT ON THE MOUND.

FINALLY, PAIGE IS READY TO PITCH. IF HE TOOK ANY WARM-UP TOSSES, I DIDN'T SEE IT.

HARD TO TELL IF PAIGE IS AWARE THAT THERE IS ANYONE ELSE IN THE STADIUM BESIDES HIMSELF.

SLOWLY, THEM BONY ARMS ARE RAISED TOWARD HEAVEN.

THEN SINK TO HIS CHEST.

THE BALL IN THE CATCHER'S MITT. PERKINS NOT MOVIN' HIS GLOVE AN INCH.

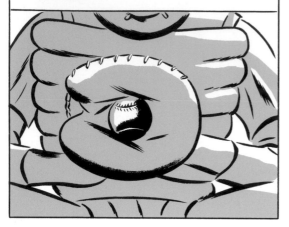

WESLEY NOT MOVIN' HIS BAT AN INCH EITHER. STRIKE ONE.

STRIKE TWO IS THE SAME PITCH, A LITTLE HIGHER IN THE STRIKE ZONE. WESLEY TAKES A CUT, MISSES BADLY.

FROM WHAT I CAN TELL, PERKINS AIN'T CALLIN' ANY PITCHES, HE JUST HOLDS OUT HIS MITT, AND PAIGE HITS IT WITH A FASTBALL.

WESLEY TRIES MOVIN' BACK IN THE BATTER'S BOX, CHOKES UP AN EXTRA INCH ON HIS BAT.

STRIKE THREE.

PAIGE WALKS AROUND THE MOUND AS INFIELDERS WHIRL THE BALL AROUND HIM.

I STEP UP TO THE PLATE.

PAIGE PAYS ME LITTLE MIND, ALL HIS ATTENTION NOW ON HIS SHOELACES.

WELL, TWO CAN PLAY AT THAT GAME. WHEN HE'S FINALLY READY TO PITCH, I CALL FOR TIME AND STEP OUT OF THE BOX.

AFTER MAKIN' PAIGE WAIT ON ME FOR A SPELL, I MOVE BACK INTO THE BOX.

I LOOK UP TO SEE PAIGE LOOKIN' AT ME, SHAKIN' HIS HEAD LIKE HE MY DADDY WAITIN' ON HIS FUSSY CHILD TO SETTLE DOWN. WHO IS HE TO SHOW ME UP LIKE THAT?

I KEEP MY HANDS LOOSE AND MY EYES LOCKED ON PAIGE'S THROWIN' HAND AS HE BEGINS HIS WINDUP.

LOTS OF MOVIN' PARTS: LEGS FLYIN' ONE WAY, ARMS ANOTHER, DISAPPEARIN' BEHIND THAT LEG, EVERYTHIN' CHUGGIN' AT A DIFFERENT SPEED.

THEN THE ARM COMES OUT AROUND, AND YOU CATCH A GLIMPSE OF THAT BALL...

LOOKS LIKE AN ASPIRIN TABLET STREAKIN' ACROSS THE PLATE, LOOKS LIKE A BASEBALL IN THE CATCHER'S MITT.

STRIKE

PAIGE'S MOUTH NOW MOVIN' AS QUICK AS HIS PITCHES.

LET HIM WORK HIS JAW -- I AIN'T GONNA GIVE HIM THE SATISFAC-TION. I TURN ASIDE.

GRIPPIN' THE BAT, I TELL MY HANDS TO RELAX. IF MY GRIP IS TOO TIGHT, MEANS I'M WOUND UP.

AIN'T A PERSON IN THIS STADIUM WHO DON'T KNOW WHAT PITCH IS COMIN'.

I START ROLLIN' THE WRISTS TO GET THE BAT MOVIN', THEN START MY SWING BEFORE I SEE THAT BALL.

I DON'T JUST CATCH UP WITH THAT FASTBALL, I *PULL* IT!

I'M HALFWAY DOWN THE FIRST-BASE LINE BEFORE I HEAR THE UMPIRE YELL, "FOUL BALL!"

PAIGE HEADS ME OFF BEFORE I GET BACK TO THE PLATE, TRYIN' TO SHAKE MY HAND, CONGRATULATIN' ME. CONGRATULATIN' ME ON A FOUL BALL!

HE PLAYIN' TO THE CROWD, SHOWIN' ME UP! WHO IS HE TO SHOW ME UP LIKE THAT!?

I PICK UP MY BAT. PERKINS SMILES AND SAYS, "THAT'S SATCHEL'S BEE BALL, NOW YOU GONNA GET HIS JUMP BALL."

I'M WOUND UP NOW AND FIXED TO SPRING. NO FASTBALL GETTIN' BY ME.

PAIGE NOW STARTS WORRYIN' OVER HIS SHOELACES!

PAIGE TAKIN' HIS TIME, MAKIN' MY BLOOD HOTTER AND HOTTER.

I'M SQUEEZIN' THE BAT LIKE I'M CHOKIN' A CHICKEN. I TRY TO CALL TIME OUT, BUT PAIGE IS ALREADY INTO HIS WINDUP.

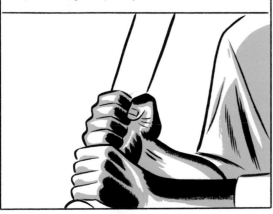

PAIGE WORKED ME UP TIGHT, ALL RIGHT. BALL IN THE CATCHER'S MITT BEFORE I COULD MOVE A MUSCLE.

LUCKY FOR ME, THE UMPIRE CALLS THE PITCH HIGH. ONE BALL, TWO STRIKES.

PAIGE NOW STARTS CLOWNIN' WITH HIS SECOND BASEMAN.

PAIGE MIGHT BEST ME TODAY, BUT I AIN'T GONNA BEAT MYSELF, HARD ENOUGH HITTIN' A BASEBALL WHEN YOU AIN'T ALL DISTRACTED.

GOT TO GET OUT OF PAIGE'S WAY OF DOIN' THINGS AND BACK TO MY OWN. I CALL FOR TIME AND STEP OUT OF THE BATTER'S BOX.

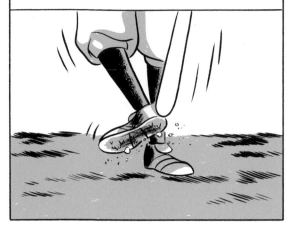

TAP MY RIGHT CLEAT THREE TIMES. FIRST TAP HARD, THEN SOFTER AND SOFTER.

SAME GOES FOR MY LEFT CLEAT.

PULL MY CAP AS LOW AS IT WILL GO, LIKE PUTTIN' BLINDERS ON A HORSE.

KEEP THE GRIP LOOSE, ROLL WRISTS, LETTIN' THE BAT HEAD KEEP A NICE EASY RHYTHM.

NO MORE THINKIN'.

CRACK

BALL RICOCHETS OFF THE SHORTSTOP'S MITT INTO SHALLOW RIGHT FIELD. SECOND BASEMAN AND RIGHT FIELDER GO AFTER IT.

I'M HARD AROUND FIRST, LOOKIN' TO GRAB SECOND.

RIGHT FIELDER BARE-HANDS IT

AND COMES UP THROWIN'.

I'M IN UNDER THE TAG. EMMET WILSON GOT HIMSELF A DOUBLE! LET THEM NEWSPAPERMEN PUT THAT IN THEIR PAPERS!

SECOND BASE MAY AS WELL BE A MOUNTAINTOP, AND I EARNED MY RIGHT TO DO SOME SHOUTIN'! I TELL PAIGE WHAT I THINK OF HIS FASTBALL! BRING ON BULLET ROGAN! I'LL TAKE 'EM ALL ON!

NOW IT'S SATCHEL THAT'S TURNIN' AWAY. I KNOCKED THEM TAIL FEATHERS RIGHT OFF THAT PEACOCK!

GEORGE McALLISTER, OUR FIRST BASEMAN, STEPS UP TO THE PLATE.

I LOOK INTO OUR DUGOUT AND SEE THE COACH GIVIN' HIS SIGNS. KNOW WITHOUT LOOKIN' WHAT IT'S GOIN' TO BE. THE BOOK ON PAIGE: BUNT AND RUN, BUNT AND RUN.

I GET ME A HEALTHY LEAD OFF SECOND.

SOON AS HE STARTS RAISIN' THEM ARMS UP, I'M OFF. I AIN'T DONE DOIN' MY DAMAGE!

PAIGE'S MOTION MIGHT BE BEDEVILIN' TO HITTERS, BUT IT'S TO THE ADVANTAGE OF BASE RUNNERS!

MAC LAYS ONE DOWN, TRYIN' TO PUSH IT BETWEEN PAIGE AND FIRST.

PAIGE IS SURPRISINGLY FAST OFF THE MOUND.

FIRES TO FIRST FOR AN OUT.

I'M AROUND THIRD, GOT NO GET-BACK IN ME NOW. HOME PLATE IS CALLIN' ME LIKE A SWOLLEN HOLLER.

FIRST BASEMAN FIRES IT HOME.

PERKINS BLOCKIN' THE PLATE, BUT I'M COMIN' WITH EVERYTHIN' I GOT.

PERKINS, THICK AND HEAVY AS A PLOW MULE, HOLDIN' THAT BALL TIGHT.

BEFORE THE UMP CAN MAKE THE CALL,
I SEE THE BALL ROLLIN' IN THE DUST.
I SCORED A RUN ON SATCHEL PAIGE!

I TRY TO RISE AND CELEBRATE.

I HEAR THE UMP. "DON'T YOU MOVE,
SON, WE GONNA GET SOME HELP."

A SHARP PAIN FILLS ME
THROUGH AND THROUGH.

THINGS START FADIN' IN AND OUT, IN AND OUT. I OPEN MY EYES AND I SEE PAIGE OVER ME, SMILIN'.

HE'S HANDIN' ME THE BASEBALL.

"HERE YOU GO, BOY, A SOUVENIR OF YOUR PLAYIN' DAYS."

1934 Dizzy Dean wins thirty games for the St. Louis Cardinals.

Paige, with his crowd-pleasing fastball, is constantly on the road, pitching for the highest bidder.

Dean finishes his amazing season by defeating the Detroit Tigers in the seventh game of the World Series.

Dean then begins a two-month barnstorming tour, pitting his all-white team against Satchel Paige's Negro All-Stars.

Touring together, they pack major league stadiums. Dean makes more money with Paige than he does all season with the Cardinals.

As they pitch against one another, Paige, more often than not, gets the better of Dean.

1935 JENNINGS FIELD, TUCKWILLA, ALABAMA ~
MR. WALKER JENNINGS IS GIVIN' HIS TWIN SONS, WALLACE AND
WILLIAM, A BIG SEND-OFF, AND WHEN MR. JENNINGS THROWS A CELEBRATION
YOU BE SMART TO ATTEND.

COLOREDS ARE NOT ALLOWED DOWN NEAR THE INFIELD AND GRANDSTAND. WE SIT OUT BY THE OUTFIELD GRASS IN THE SHADE OF CARPENTER WOODS. CLOSEST I CAME TO A BASEBALL FIELD SINCE MY KNEE QUIT ON ME.

MY MOMMA WORKED IN THE JENNINGS'S HOME. WASHED THEM BOYS' CLOTHING, COOKED THEM THEIR FOOD, SAW MORE OF THEM LITTLE BOYS THAN SHE DID ME.

FROM WHERE WE AT YOU COULDN'T HEAR MR. JENNINGS'S SPEECH, BUT THE WHOLE TOWN KNOWS WHAT IT IS ABOUT. THE JENNINGS BOYS ARE TAKIN' THE EVENING TRAIN TO MISSOURI. THEY HAVE A TRYOUT WITH THE WORLD CHAMPION ST. LOUIS CARDINALS.

THEM TWINS GOOD. I WAS BETTER.

WHEN MR. JENNINGS FINISHES HIS SPEECH, EVERYBODY WHOOPS AND HOLLERS. THE BAND CLIMBS ONTO THE GAZEBO AND STRIKES UP "MEET ME IN ST. LOUIS."

MR. WALLACE WALKS ONTO THE FIELD AND PICKS UP THE BAT THAT WAS SITTING ON HOME PLATE.

MR. WILLIAM JOGS OUT PAST THE PITCHER'S MOUND, PAST SECOND BASE, AND INTO CENTER FIELD WHERE A BUCKET OF BASEBALLS WAITS FOR HIM.

MR. WILLIAM GOES INTO HIS WINDUP. HE'S GOIN' TO PITCH FROM OUT THERE, MORE THAN 200 FEET FROM THE PLATE.

NO CATCHER SETS UP BEHIND HOME PLATE.

EVERY PITCH COMES RIGHT DOWN MAIN STREET.

MR. WALLACE HITS EVERY PITCH, SPRAYIN' THE BALL ALL OVER THE FIELD. EACH BALL IS HIT FARTHER THAN THE ONE BEFORE.

THE LAST PITCH IS HIT THE HARDEST.

UP OVER THE OUTFIELD AND INTO CARPENTER WOODS -- THAT BALL MUST HAVE TRAVELED OVER 450 FEET.

MY SON EMMET, JR. AND ANOTHER HALF DOZEN CHILDREN RACE INTO THEM WOODS LOOKIN' FOR THAT BALL.

ONE OF THE BOYS COME OUTTA THE WOODS WITH THAT BASEBALL. THEY ALL COULDN'T HAVE BEEN MORE EXCITED IF THEY'D DISCOVERED BURIED TREASURE.

ONLY BASEBALL A COLORED BOY KNOWS IS A WASHRAG TIED AROUND A ROCK. EVEN SOME OF THE ADULTS GATHER ROUND TO TAKE A LOOK.

ALL OF A SUDDEN, A LOUD WHISTLE.

IT'S MR. JENNINGS HIMSELF MAKIN' HIS WAY TOWARD US.

HE HOLDS OUT HIS HAND...

AND COLLECTS HIS BALL.

1941 Satchel Paige is the greatest box office attraction in baseball. Receiving a percentage of ticket sales, he is also the world's highest-paid athlete. Paige now takes to flying from game to game aboard a private DC-3 airplane.

National press coverage in LIFE and TIME introduces Paige to an even greater audience. White major league hitters, including Rogers Hornsby, Hack Wilson, Ted Williams, and Joe DiMaggio regard Paige as the toughest pitcher they ever faced.

Yet despite his success, Paige cannot play in the major leagues because he is black. Said Paige: "All the nice statements in the world ain't gonna knock down Jim Crow."

1942 IN JANUARY, MR. WALKER JENNINGS PASSES ON.

ALL OF TUCKWILLA ATTENDS HIS FUNERAL.

HIS TWIN SONS, LONG RETURNED FROM PLAYIN' TWO YEARS FOR A CARDINALS MINOR LEAGUE TEAM, CLAIM THEIR INHERITANCE.

MR. JENNINGS WASN'T A WARMHEARTED MAN, BUT YOU ALWAYS KNEW WHERE YOU STOOD. WHEN HIS FENCE BROKE AND HIS STOCK STARTED EATIN' MY CROP, HE'D FIX THAT FENCE RIGHT AWAY.

THEM BOYS WILL LET THEIR STOCK EAT ALL YOUR GARDEN UP BEFORE THEY GET OFF THEIR HORSES AND FIX WHAT BELONGS TO THEM.

SO I FIX THEIR FENCE MYSELF.

THEM JENNINGS TWINS DO NOTHIN' FOR YOU EXCEPT GET INTO YOUR BUSINESS LOOKING FOR FAULTS AND FAILURES.

"YOU MAKIN' THOSE ROWS WIDE ENOUGH? FOUR FEET?"

FOUR FEET ON THIS THIN LAND? YOU CAN'T GO FOUR FEET ON THIS THIN LAND.

DURIN' PLANTIN': "YOU LAYIN' DOWN TOO MUCH FERTILIZER, EMMET."

EVEN MY BOY KNOWS IF YOU DON'T LAY DOWN ENOUGH GUANO, YOUR COTTON DON'T GET UP AND GET.

I JUST HUMBLE DOWN: "THAT'S SOMETHIN' TO THINK ABOUT, MR. WILLIAM."

THEN I JUST KEEP ON DOIN' THINGS THE WAY I KNOW HOW TO DO THEM.

SOON AS THAT COTTON IS READY TO BE PICKED, THE TUCKWILLA SCHOOL BOARD ALWAYS RUNS OUT OF MONEY.

NEVER SHUT DOWN THE WHITE SCHOOL. ALWAYS ENOUGH MONEY TO KEEP THEM OPEN. NEGRO EDUCATION BE DAMNED.

WE TAKE UP A COLLECTION FOR THE TEACHER TO KEEP TEACHIN'. SOME YEARS IT AIN'T MORE THAN CORN, CABBAGE, AND SIDE MEAT.

AIN'T GONNA KEEP MY BOY DOWN LIKE THAT AS LONG AS THERE'S A TEACHER WILLIN' TO TEACH.

ON A GOOD DAY I CAN PUT 100 LBS. OF COTTON IN A SACK. FRANCES, MY COUSINS FLOYD AND BUSTER, THEY HELP OUT TOO.

THEM JENNINGS TWINS, THEY KEEP COMIN'
ROUND. "WHERE YOUR BOY AT, EMMET?"

"GETTIN' HIS LESSONS, MR. WILLIAM."

I STAY SHUT MOUTHED AND KEEP PICKIN'
AND SAY NO MORE ABOUT THE MATTER.

THE NEXT DAY THE JENNINGS TWINS CATCH UP WITH EMMET, JR. AND A FEW OF
HIS PALS OVER BY WICKAHIKEN CREEK AND CALL IT TRESPASSIN'. THEM TWINS
OWN MOST OF TUCKWILLA -- WALKIN' OUT YOUR DOOR IS TRESPASSIN' IF THEY
CHOOSE TO CALL IT THAT.

THEY CAME DOWN OFF THEIR HORSES AND TOOK A STRAP TO THEM BOYS.

EMMET, JR. COME HOME ALL ROUGHED UP. FRANCES IS SCARED. WHAT HAPPENED TO LUCAS CRUTCHFIELD IS STILL FRESH IN EVERYONE'S MIND.

NEXT DAY THEY BACK. "WHERE YOUR BOY AT, EMMET? BOY RAISED RIGHT SHOULD BE HELPIN' HIS DADDY."

I DON'T TAKE OFF MY HAT. I MENTION NOTHING ABOUT HIS LESSONS, EITHER. "BE JOININ' ME SOON, MR. WALLACE."

I HUMBLE DOWN AGAIN, BUT KEEP ON DOIN' THINGS THE WAY I SEE BEST TO DO THEM.

NEXT FEW DAYS THE TWINS COME ROUND, THEY KEEP THEIR DISTANCE AND I KEEP MINE. I KNOW WHAT THEY WAITIN' TO SEE.

FEW MORE DAYS PASS LIKE THIS TILL FINALLY THEY RIDE OVER.

"WHERE YOUR BOY AT, EMMET?"

THERE WAS PLENTY OF ANGER IN ME BUT I HOLD MY TONGUE. WHAT ELSE WAS I TO DO? CRY ABOUT MY RIGHTS? TELL THEM I AM BEIN' MISTREATED?

YOU DO THAT, AND YOU DIE NO DIFFERENT THAN LUCAS CRUTCHFIELD.

TUESDAY THE FOLLOWING WEEK, EMMET, JR. IS COMING HOME AFTER FETCHING A FEW FRYERS FROM ELMER BETTIS FOR OUR DINNER.

BY THE TIME EMMET, JR. SAW 'EM, IT WAS TOO LATE. HE DIDN'T MAKE IT HOME IN TIME FOR DINNER.

FRANCES KNEW RIGHT AWAY THAT SOMETHIN' WAS TERRIBLY WRONG. BOY WASN'T EVEN AN HOUR LATE, AND SHE KNEW.

I HEADED TOWARD ELMER'S PLACE AS FAST AS MY GIMPY LEG WOULD CARRY ME.

"EMMET, JR. COME AND GONE ABOUT TWO HOURS AGO," ELMER SAYS.

I MAKE A FEW MORE INQUIRIES, BUT NO ONE HAD SEEN EMMET, JR.

I HEADED HOME AND SAW CECIL BROWN'S WAGON PARKED OUT FRONT. SOMETHIN' IRREGULAR GOIN' ON, CECIL BROWN NEVER CALLED ON US BEFORE. HE NOT THE VISITIN' TYPE.

CECIL WAS RIDIN' RIGHT PAST CARSON CROSSING AND SAW ONE OF THEM FRYERS LAYIN' IN THE ROAD.

THEN HE HEARD SOME RUSTLIN' IN THE GRASS. THOUGHT IT WAS A FOX OR MAYBE A WILD PIG. HE GOT OFF HIS WAGON TO TAKE A LOOK.

HE FOUND EMMET, JR. WITH HIS HANDS TRUSSED BEHIND HIS BACK AND A COTTON SACK TIED AROUND HIS HEAD. BLOOD LEAKIN' THROUGH THE SACK.

FOR THE REST OF THE EVENIN'
THINGS WERE REAL QUIET
AROUND THE HOUSE.

FRANCES AND I HARDLY SPOKE
A WORD BETWEEN US WHILE SHE
TENDED TO EMMET, JR.

HIS INJURIES WEREN'T AS BAD AS
WE'D FEARED. MOST OF THE BLOOD
BELONGED TO THE CHICKEN.

NEXT TIME, THAT MIGHT NOT BE
THE CASE.

NEXT MORNIN', EMMET, JR. JOINS ME IN THE FIELD PICKIN' COTTON.

1943 EACH AND EVERY SUNDAY MORNIN' SINCE I STOPPED PLAYIN' BALL, FRANCES INSISTED I ATTEND CHURCH. SHE WORRIES ABOUT ME IN THIS LIFE AND THE NEXT.

I LISTEN TO PASTOR WILLS PREACHIN', I HEAR THE SPIRITUALS. I SEE THEM WORDS AND THEM HYMNS TOUCHIN' PEOPLE ON THE INSIDE. BUT THEY DON'T TOUCH MY INSIDE.

EACH AND EVERY SUNDAY, THE CONGREGATION WALKS DOWN TO THE RIVER. EACH AND EVERY WEEK, PASTOR WILLS SHOUTS OUT, "WHO WILL BE CLEANSED BY JESUS? WHO WILL LET JESUS WASH AWAY THEIR TROUBLES? WHO WILL LET JESUS WASH AWAY ALL THEIR PAIN AND ANGER?"

EACH AND EVERY WEEK I STAY PUT.

IF THE RIVER WASHED AWAY ALL MY PAIN AND ANGER, THERE WOULD BE NOTHING LEFT.

1944

BASEBALL

SATCHEL PAIGE ALL-STARS

— VS. —

TUCKWILLA ALL-STARS

SATURDAY, SEPT. 2
AT 2:00 P.M.

JENNINGS PARK

CHILDREN 20¢ ADULTS 50¢

FEATURING PITCHING LEGEND SATCHEL PAIGE

NEVER SEEN A CROWD SO BIG IN TUCKWILLA. THEY'RE COMIN' FROM AS FAR AWAY AS
DANVILLE AND LYME. EMMET, JR., LIKE EVERY BLACK BOY IN ALABAMA, WORSHIPS
SATCHEL PAIGE.

FRANCES WAS GOIN' TO BRING EMMET, JR. HERE TODAY--THEN HER SISTER TOOK
ILL AND SHE HAD TO CARE FOR HER. I WOULD NOT HAVE BEEN HERE OTHERWISE.
BASEBALL REMINDS ME OF THINGS I'D RATHER NOT THINK ABOUT.

BOY HAS SOME NOTION THAT I ONCE PLAYED BALL, BUT HE DIDN'T HEAR IT FROM ME.
I DON'T TALK ABOUT MY DAYS AS A BALLPLAYER. IT'S LIKE TALKIN' ABOUT A
DEAD MAN.

SATCHEL PAIGE ALL STARS

THEM TWINS SPENT A FEW DOLLARS TRYIN' TO MAKE JENNINGS FIELD INTO A REAL BALLPARK, SHADED GRANDSTAND FOR WHITES AND A DUGOUT FOR THE HOME TEAM.

EVERYONE TURNIN' OUT TODAY, EVEN CLARA COLES, OLDEST PERSON IN ALL OF TUCKWILLA.

EMMET, JR. AND I FIND US A SEAT.

NO SIGN OF PAIGE, BUT THE REST OF HIS TEAM IS HERE. SOME OF 'EM STRETCHIN' OUT, OTHERS CATCHIN' A FEW WINKS, LIKELY TIRED FROM AN ALL-NIGHT BUS RIDE. THEY ALL LOOK FAMILIAR, BUT I DON'T RECOGNIZE ANY OF 'EM.

49

TUCKWILLA TEAM IS ON THE FIELD, WARMIN' UP, THEM I RECOGNIZE.

THE TWINS, OF COURSE.

CHRISTIAN DOOLEY OWNS THE LUMBER MILL. HOWARD GIBBS IS THE SHERIFF.

OSCAR OWENS, HE HERE TOO. HE AIN'T FROM TUCKWILLA, BORN AND RAISED IN MOBILE.

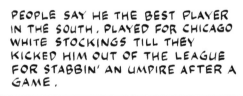
PEOPLE SAY HE THE BEST PLAYER IN THE SOUTH. PLAYED FOR CHICAGO WHITE STOCKINGS TILL THEY KICKED HIM OUT OF THE LEAGUE FOR STABBIN' AN UMPIRE AFTER A GAME.

JUST ABOUT GAME TIME, AND STILL NO SIGN OF PAIGE. HIS TEAM TAKES THE FIELD FOR THEIR WARM-UPS.

A BATTER HITS A BALL TO THE INFIELDERS, STARTIN' WITH THE THIRD BASEMAN.

HE MAKES THE PLAY, DIVIN' TO HIS RIGHT ...

AND COMES UP THROWIN' FROM HIS KNEES,

THE FIRST BASEMAN, STRETCHIN' ABOUT AS FAR AS HE CAN GO, SCOOPS UP THE THROW OUT OF THE DIRT,

ALL THE INFIELDERS GET INTO THE ACT NOW: BARE-HANDED PICKUPS...

SOMERSAULTIN' THROWS... EMMET, JR, IS AMAZED BY THE ACROBATICS,

I POINT OUT THEY JUST PUTTIN' ON A SHOW, PLAYIN' SHADOW BALL -- BASEBALL WITHOUT A BALL.

"THEY JUST TRICKIN' YOU, BOY. IT AIN'T REAL."

JENNINGS TWINS, THEY AIN'T AMUSED, THEY WEARIN' THEIR GAME FACES.

THEY HEAD OVER TO HOME PLATE TO HAVE A WORD WITH THE BATTER. THEY SURELY PAID A PRETTY PENNY TO GET PAIGE HERE, AND THEY WANT TO KNOW WHERE HE AT.

A HALF HOUR PASSES.

WITH A CROWD GROWIN' RESTLESS AND THE TWINS NOT WANTIN' TO REFUND ANY TICKETS, THEY DECIDE TO START WITHOUT PAIGE.

MAE BELLOWS AND MARION WERTH, TUCKWILLA'S TWO WHITE WAR WIDOWS, STAND AT HOME PLATE AND SING THE NATIONAL ANTHEM.

WILLIAM JENNINGS TAKES THE MOUND AND KICKS THE DIRT THIS WAY AND THAT, GETTIN' IT JUST SO.

TAKES A FEW WARM-UP PITCHES.

THE COLORED TEAM LEAD HITTER STANDS A FEW FEET FROM THE PLATE, TAKIN' SOME SWINGS.

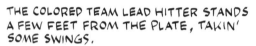

GAME YET TO BEGIN AND EMMET, JR.'S EYES GLUED TO THAT BASEBALL DIAMOND. IT'S MORE THAN THE BIG CROWD THAT HAS HIM EXCITED.

FOR THE FIRST TIME IN HIS LIFE, HE SEEIN' A BLACK MAN GOIN' HEAD-TO-HEAD WITH A WHITE MAN. NOT JUST ANY WHITE MAN EITHER, BUT ONE OF THE JENNINGS TWINS.

THE UMPIRE YELLS, "PLAY BALL!"

LEADOFF HITTER, SHORT FELLA, STEPS INTO BATTER'S BOX. BATS LEFTY.

TAKES THE FIRST PITCH. "STRIKE ONE."

HOMETOWN UMP HAS A GENEROUS STRIKE ZONE. NEXT PITCH IS INSIDE AND IS ALSO CALLED A STRIKE.

HITTER, WITH TWO STRIKES ON HIM, NOW STARTS SWINGIN' AT ANYTHIN' CLOSE, FOULS OFF TWO PITCHES.

CRACK

ON THE FIFTH PITCH HE GOES DOWN SWINGIN'.

BASEBALL IS WON AND LOST ON THE LITTLE THINGS, DETAILS THAT MOST PEOPLE WON'T EVER NOTICE UNLESS THEY LOOKIN' FOR IT. LIKE A HITTER CHOKIN' UP ON THE BAT AFTER TWO STRIKES,

OR HOW A PITCHER MAY TELEGRAPH HIS PITCHES BY DIPPIN' A SHOULDER OR THE WAY HE GRIPS A BALL.

AS THE GAME GOES ON, I START POINTIN' THESE THINGS OUT TO MY BOY, AND BEFORE I REALIZE IT, I AM PULLED BACK INTO THE GAME. IT'S LIKE FEELIN' A LIMB THAT YOU THOUGHT YOU LOST.

IN THE SECOND INNING, NEGRO TEAM LEADOFF MAN DRAGS A BUNT.

THEN A HIT-AND-RUN. SHORTSTOP COVERS SECOND AND THE GROUND BALL IS SMACKED RIGHT WHERE HE USUALLY AT.

RUNNER GOIN' ALL THE WAY TO THIRD ON THE PLAY.

NEXT, A DELAYED DOUBLE STEAL. CATCHER THROWS TO SECOND.

RUNNER SLIDES IN SAFE AS BALL BOUNCES OFF HIS SHOULDER.

RUNNER ON THIRD COMES HOME TO SCORE.

NEXT BATTER PUSHES A GROUNDER TO SECOND. IT'S THE FIRST OUT, BUT IT ALLOWS THE RUNNER ON SECOND TO MOVE OVER TO THIRD.

NEXT BATTER HITS A POP FLY TO THE CENTER FIELDER FOR THE SECOND OUT.

THE RUNNER ON THIRD TAGS AND SCORES -- TWO RUNS ON A COUPLE OF WEAK SINGLES! THAT'S THE NEGRO GAME! FASTER, MORE AGGRESSIVE THAN THE WHITE GAME.

IN THE FOURTH INNING, TUCKWILLA STARTS FLEXIN' THEIR MUSCLES.

AFTER TWO OUTS, DOOLEY RIPS A DOUBLE DOWN THE LINE...

MR. WALLACE GETS A HOLD OF ONE NEXT.

HITS A MAMMOTH HOME RUN.

OUTFIELDERS DON'T BOTHER TO GO BACK ON IT. THEY KNOW IT'S GONE.

MR. WILLIAM UP NEXT.

HE TEARS INTO THAT BALL AND SENDS IT INTO THE CORNER FOR A STAND-UP DOUBLE.

COLORED PITCHER STARTIN' TO DROOP WITH TUCKWILLA'S BEST HITTER STEPPIN' UP.

OSCAR OWENS.

FIRST PITCH TO HIM IS HIT OFF THE TOP OF THE BAT AND HIT A MILE HIGH.

THE SHORTSTOP STARTS IMMEDIATELY SCREAMIN', "I GOT IT! I GOT IT!"

MR. WILLIAM HESITATES FOR A MOMENT AT SECOND BASE...

...AS THE BALL BOUNCES OFF THE OUTFIELD FENCE AND IS PLAYED BY THE LEFT FIELDER.

MR. WILLIAM, REALIZIN' HE BEEN TRICKED, NOW TAKES OFF.

LEFT FIELDER GETS RID OF IT QUICK AS MR. WILLIAM, NOW IN FULL STRIDE, IS AROUND THIRD HEADIN' FOR HOME.

THE THROW EASILY BEATS MR. WILLIAM...

WHO'S COMIN' INTO HOME HARD, HOPIN' TO KNOCK THE BALL LOOSE.

THUD

CATCHER HOLDS ON TO THE BALL, AND THE INNING IS OVER.

THE NEXT FEW INNINGS ARE PLAYED HARD. MR. WILLIAM PITCHIN' BATTERS INSIDE AND TIGHT.

WHEN THE SHORTSTOP WHO FOOLED HIM COMES TO BAT, HE GETS PLUNKED WITH A FASTBALL.

SHORTSTOP GOT NO GET-BACK IN HIM! HE STEALS SECOND AND THIRD!

MR. WILLIAM, THOUGH, HE GETTIN' STRONGER AS THE GAME GOES ON. STRIKES OUT THE SIDE.

ENTERING THE BOTTOM OF THE EIGHTH INNING, TUCKWILLA IS DOWN 6 RUNS TO 3. HOW I WANT TO SEE THAT SCORE HOLD.

	1	2	3	4	5	6	7	8	9		
VISITORS	0	2	1	2	0	0	1	0			6
TUCKWILLA	0	0	0	2	0	1	0				3

THE COLORED PITCHER AIN'T GETTIN' THE SAME MOVEMENT ON HIS PITCHES...

...AND TUCKWILLA IS HITTIN' HIM HARD,

THE FIRST THREE BATTERS ALL GET HITS,

THE FIRST HITTER IS COMIN' AROUND TO SCORE,

KEEP EXPECTIN' THE PITCHER TO BE PULLED, BUT AS DROOPY AS HE IS, HE STAYS IN THE GAME, IT'S LIKELY THE TEAM PROBABLY PLAYED A DOUBLEHEADER YESTERDAY AND HAS ANOTHER GAME TONIGHT, TEAM AIN'T GONNA WASTE ANOTHER ARM ON THIS GAME.

BATTER STEPS UP TO THE PLATE.

FIRST PITCH AIN'T NEAR THE STRIKE ZONE.

THE SECOND PITCH IS IN THE DIRT, THE CATCHER MAKES A GOOD PLAY TO KEEP THE BALL FROM GETTIN' PAST 'EM.

THIRD PITCH IS A BREAKIN' BALL THAT DON'T BREAK.

ANOTHER RUN SCORES. TUCKWILLA IS WITHIN' ONE, AND STILL NO OUTS.

HOWARD GIBBS STEPS INTO THE BATTER'S BOX. HE SMELLS BLOOD AND IS READY TO TAKE HIS CUTS.

BUT THE PITCHER, HE AIN'T LOOKIN' AT THE CATCHER'S MITT.

NO ONE AT JENNINGS FIELD IS LOOKIN' AT THE BATTER OR THE PITCHER.

ALL EYES ARE ON THE MAIN ENTRANCE BY THE GRANDSTAND.

SATCHEL PAIGE HAS ARRIVED.

PAIGE WORKS THE MOUND TO HIS LIKIN'...

GIBBS AND THE UMPIRE WAITIN' ON PAIGE TO TAKE HIS WARM-UPS, CATCHER IN HIS CROUCH,

PAIGE DON'T MOVE, HE WAITIN' ON THE BATTER, HE READY TO PITCH!

STRIKE ONE!

NEXT PITCH SAME AS THE FIRST, MAYBE A HAIR OUTSIDE.

UMP CALLS IT A BALL.

PAIGE SMILES EAR-TO-EAR, STEPS OFF THE MOUND AND HAS A FEW WORDS FOR THE UMP. ANOTHER FIRST FOR EMMET, JR.: SEEIN' A BLACK MAN SASS A WHITE.

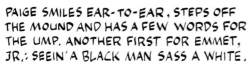

AFTER JAWIN' FOR ANOTHER MINUTE, PAIGE STEPS BACK ONTO THE MOUND.

AIN'T A PERSON IN THE CROWD NOT PAYIN' ATTENTION. ANYTHIN' IS NOW POSSIBLE.

THE NEXT PITCH IS A BIG BREAKIN' CURVEBALL THAT IS SWUNG AT AND MISSED. ONE BALL, TWO STRIKES.

PAIGE'S NEXT PITCH IS ANOTHER FAST-BALL, AND GIBBS STROKES IT BETWEEN THIRD AND SHORT.

A RUN COMES IN, AND THE GAME IS TIED.

THE TUCKWILLA DUGOUT CELEBRATIN'!

PAIGE DON'T SEEM PARTICULARLY BOTHERED BY IT. HE WALKS OVER TO FIRST BASE TO CONGRATULATE GIBBS FOR GETTIN' A HIT OFF HIM.

GIBBS NEVER SHOOK A BLACK MAN'S HAND BEFORE, AND HE AIN'T STARTIN' NOW.

NEXT HITTER IS DOOLEY.

PAIGE'S FIRST PITCH IS A FASTBALL RIGHT BY HIM.

NEXT PITCH IS ANOTHER ONE.

THIS ONE IS HIT, THOUGH.

THE THIRD BASEMAN STABS AT IT, BUT IT RICOCHETS OFF THE HEEL OF HIS GLOVE.

THE SHORTSTOP QUICKLY COLLECTS THE BALL IN SHALLOW LEFT FIELD, TOO LATE TO MAKE A PLAY AT FIRST.

BASES ARE LOADED, AND BOTH BATTERS WHO FACED PAIGE HAVE GOTTEN HITS OFF HIM. PAIGE MAY NOT LOOK ANY OLDER, BUT HE AIN'T GOT NEAR THE SAME FASTBALL HE ONCE DID. I CAN'T HELP BUT WONDER IF THIS MAN CAN STILL PITCH, OR IF HE JUST ALL SHOW.

SOME TAUNTIN' COMIN' FROM THE TUCKWILLA BENCH. IF PAIGE HEARS, IT DON'T BOTHER HIM NONE.

HE STILL LOOKIN' FOR LAUGHS. HE WALKS OVER TO THE THIRD BASEMAN. PAIGE CHECKS TO SEE IF THERE'S A HOLE IN HIS MITT.

MR. WALLACE STEPS UP TO THE PLATE.

RUNNERS TAKE THEIR LEAD OFF THE BASES.

PAIGE HASN'T TAKEN THE MOUND--HE STILL JAWIN' TO HIS THIRD BASEMAN. JUST AS I REMEMBER, EVERYTHIN' REVOLVIN' AROUND PAIGE. HOWEVER BIG THE GAME, PAIGE IS BIGGER.

MR. WALLACE, HE GETTIN' STEAMED! BARKS SOMETHIN' AT PAIGE.

PAIGE HAS GOT HIS GOAT! COLORED SECTION HOOTIN' AND LAUGHIN'.

PAIGE STEPS TOWARD THE PLATE. STILL PLAYIN' THINGS FOR LAUGHS. PRETENDS HE CAN'T HEAR.

MR. WALLACE WALKS A FOOT TOWARD THE MOUND.

HE YELLS AGAIN. THIS TIME IT IS LOUD ENOUGH FOR EVERYONE TO HEAR.

PITCH THE BALL, YOU WASHED-UP NIGGER!

PAIGE TURNS HIS BACK TO THE PLATE AND GESTURES TO HIS FIELDERS.

THE OUTFIELDERS JOG IN...

AND TAKE A SEAT WITH THE INFIELDERS BEHIND SECOND BASE.

PAIGE RECLAIMS THE MOUND.

THE CATCHER SQUATS BEHIND THE PLATE.

MR. WALLACE HESITATES BEFORE STEPPIN' INTO THE BATTER'S BOX, AND EXCHANGES WORDS WITH HIS BROTHER IN THE ON-DECK CIRCLE.

MR. WILLIAM SHOUTS SOMETHIN' AT THE MOUND.

WHATEVER WAS SAID, PAIGE DON'T ACKNOWLEDGE IT. CLOWNIN' TIME IS OVER, HE ALL BUSINESS NOW.

TUCKWILLA DUGOUT IS ON ITS FEET KICKIN' UP A FUSS, THINKIN' PAIGE IS PLAYIN' MORE GAMES. WHAT THEY SHOUTIN', I'D RATHER NOT REPEAT.

PAIGE JUST WAITS.

MR. WALLACE STEPS INTO THE BATTER'S BOX, REFUSIN' TO BE SHOWN UP. ALL HE HAS TO DO IS PUT THE BALL IN PLAY, AND EVERY RUN SCORES.

THAT BALL WAS MOVIN' SO FAST I COULDN'T EVEN SEE IT. IF I DIDN'T KNOW BETTER, I'D A THOUGHT THEY WAS PLAYIN' SHADOW BALL.

NEXT PITCH SAME AS THE FIRST.

MR. WALLACE GOES DOWN ON THREE PITCHES.

PAIGE GETS THE BALL BACK AND WASTES NO TIME GETTIN' READY.

MR. WILLIAM STEPS UP TO THE PLATE.

THREE MORE PITCHES,
AND MR. WILLIAM STRIKES OUT
JUST LIKE HIS BROTHER.

NEXT BATTER, OSCAR OWENS, STANDS IN.

AFTER TAKIN' A PITCH FOR A STRIKE, HE TRIES TO BUNT.

YOU KNOW YOU LICKED WHEN YOUR CLEANUP HITTER IS BUNTIN'. OWENS NEVER MAKES CONTACT. GOES DOWN ON THREE PITCHES TOO. INNING OVER.

WHOOSH!

THE CROWD IS ON THEIR FEET, CHEERIN'. NOT JUST THE COLORED SECTION, EITHER.

PAIGE AIN'T JAWIN' NO MORE,
IN NINE PITCHES HE SAID WHAT HE HAD TO SAY.

THE LAST INNIN' IS AN AFTERTHOUGHT. DON'T ASK ME THE FINAL SCORE. I COULDN'T TELL YOU.

PAIGE DOESN'T EVEN RETURN TO THE MOUND IN THE NINTH. BY THE TIME THE GAME ENDED, HE WAS PROBABLY WELL ON HIS WAY TO THE NEXT GAME, HIS NEXT PAYCHECK, TUCKWILLA JUST ANOTHER GIG.

EMMET, JR. AND I WALKED HOME TOGETHER, MY BOY AS SPIRITED AS I'VE SEEN HIM FOR SOME TIME, STOPPIN' EVERY SO OFTEN TO APE SATCHEL'S HERKY-JERKY WINDUP.

I'M STILL LIMPIN' ALONG, BUT I GOT A BOUNCE IN MY STEP, TOO.

I THOUGHT HARD ABOUT THEM JENNINGS TWINS, HOW IT CAME TO BE THAT THESE MEN LORDED OVER US. HOW DO MEN SO SMALL GET SO LARGE? WHO MADE IT SO?

YOU LIVE UNDER THEIR RULIN' FOR SO LONG THAT YOU SOON FORGET WHO YOU ARE, WHAT YOU CAN BE.

THAT EVENIN' AFTER SUPPER, EMMET, JR. AND I RETIRED TO THE PORCH, AND I SHOWED HIM SOMETHIN' I HAD HID AWAY FOR MANY YEARS.

IT WAS THE BASEBALL GIVEN TO ME BY SATCHEL PAIGE.

FOR THE FIRST TIME, I TOLD EMMET, JR. THE STORY OF HOW HIS DADDY WENT HEAD-TO-HEAD WITH SATCHEL PAIGE.

AND UNLIKE THEM TUCKWILLA BOYS,

HIS DADDY CAME OUT ON TOP.

CRACK

FOR THE FIRST TIME SINCE I PLAYED BALL, SINCE EMMET, JR. WAS A BABY, I FELT SOMETHIN' ON THE INSIDE. I REMEMBERED THE TYPE OF MAN I AM.

I GAVE EMMET, JR. THAT BALL ... I HOPE IT REMINDS HIM OF WHO HE CAN BE.

THE END

Striking Out Jim Crow
Panel Discussions

 **PAGE 1:** *Wages*
In 1929, black sharecroppers earned about forty to fifty cents a day. A maid, working seven days a week, might bring in four dollars for the week. Some of the better Negro League ballplayers were paid $275 per month. That's what Paige made playing for the Birmingham Black Barons in 1929. After the stock market crash of 1929, signaling the Great Depression, these wages fell.

 **PAGE 2:** *The Railroad*
From 1900 to 1945 was the Golden Age of the railroad. Ninety-eight percent of all travel between cities in 1916 was by train. It wasn't until the 1930s that the automobile cut into the rail passenger market.

By 1920, 100,000 travelers per night were sleeping in Pullman sleepers. The Pullman Company was the largest employer of Negroes in America. The service provided by the African American Pullman porters was legendary and within African American communities the Pullman porters were held in high regard. In 1937, the Brotherhood of Sleeping Car Porters, under the leadership of A. Philip Randolph, was finally recognized as the porters' official union by the Pullman Company after a long and often bitter struggle. Their fight for better working conditions helped lay the foundation for the civil rights movement.

The sound of a locomotive's whistle could be heard in the homes of most Americans. Lumber, steel, refrigerators, milk, newspapers—the railroad shipped almost every product consumed in America. A train whistle might also signal the arrival of the circus, traveling theater shows, vaudeville acts, and, of course, sports teams.

 **PAGE 2:** *Sharecropper Shacks*
Poorly constructed sharecropper shacks were usually built on the landowner's property and leased back to the sharecropper. Rent was subtracted from the sharecropper's wages. Landowners would also charge for use of tools, equipment, and even food. Despite working the land the whole year, the sharecropper would often find himself in debt to the landowner.

PAGE 3: *The Negro National League*
The Negro National League was the first all-black league to last more than one season. It was started in 1920 by Rube Foster, former star pitcher and owner-manager of the Chicago American Giants. In 1929, the league included the Chicago American Giants, Cuban Stars, Detroit Stars, Kansas City Monarchs, Burmingham Black Barons, and Memphis Red Sox. The league folded in 1931, another victim of the Great Depression.

 **PAGE 4:** *African American Press*
If you were looking in the 1920s for articles about black businesses, sports figures, or cultural figures, you'd find virtually no mention of them in the majority of newspapers. Like the rest of the country, the newspaper industry was segregated. The *Chicago Defender*, *Pittsburgh Courier*, and the Baltimore *Afro-American* were three of the country's most widely circulated black newspapers. The newspapers were read throughout the country. Black Pullman porters carried the papers south across the Mason-Dixon Line. The papers advocated for better working and living conditions for blacks throughout the country.

The sports pages in African American papers fought for integration years before Jackie Robinson broke baseball's color barrier in 1947.

shortstop Derek Jeter compulsively tugged at both his batting gloves as he stepped out of the batter's box between every pitch of an at-bat.

PAGE 4: *Bullet Rogan*
It was not until he was thirty, after more than nine years of playing on U.S. Army teams, that Wilber "Bullet" Joe Rogan began his Negro Leagues career with the Kansas City Monarchs. His devastating fastball, along with a dazzling array of forkballs, palm balls, spitballs, and curves, made him one of the League's most dominant pitchers. Rogan also played as an outfielder and led the Negro National League in 1922 with sixteen home runs.

PAGE 5: *Paige's Personal Catcher*
Albany, Georgia, native Bill Perkins was Satchel Paige's personal catcher throughout his career. He was a strong defensive catcher and wore a chest protector emblazoned with the words *Thou shalt not steal!* As Satchel jumped from team to team, he would insist that Perkins be signed along with him. In 1948, the year Paige made it to the major leagues, Perkins was shot and killed in a restaurant.

PAGE 13: *Paige's Pitches*
Paige was a brilliant self-promoter. He even promoted his pitches by giving them names! They included the Jump Ball, Bee Ball, Hesitation, Nothing Ball, Hurry-up Ball, Drop Ball, Bat Dodger, the Midnight Creeper, and Four-day Rider.

Page 15: *Rituals and Rhythms*
Ballplayers from all sports often engage in rituals and routines as a way to combat distractions and focus their attention. For example, a basketball player, before shooting a free throw, may always lift a hand toward the basket and then dribble the ball three times. The Yankee all-star

PAGE 19: *Speed and Daring*
The Negro League games, as opposed to those of the white major leagues, stressed aggressive base running. Teams did not sit around waiting for home runs but rather forced the action with hit-and-runs, suicide squeezes, and double steals. Opposing teams felt that Satchel Paige's delivery made it easy to steal bases. As a power pitcher with a high leg kick, he gave runners more of a head start when they were trying to swipe a base.

PAGE 24: *Barnstorming*
Barnstorming was a popular form of entertainment in the 1920s, in which stunt pilots would perform tricks with airplanes, flying from town to town, often landing in farmers' fields by the barns. The term *barnstorming* also became linked with sports teams, especially baseball. Teams caravaned by motorcar or bus over dirt roads, traveling hundreds of miles each day. Day games were often followed by a night game in the next county, followed by a doubleheader the next afternoon 500 miles away.

Life on the road was rough going for black barnstormers. Most hotels wouldn't give them rooms, forcing them to sleep on buses, in barns, or in stadiums. Players would travel to play exhibition games against white and other black teams to earn extra income beyond what their teams paid them. The games against whites were cash cows, often drawing thousands of fans to these small towns to witness the great Negro League players.

PAGES 24, 26: *The 1934 St. Louis Cardinals*
In 1934, the St. Louis Cardinals were the Major League Baseball World Series champions. Their nickname was "The Gas House Gang," due to the team's generally shabby appearance and rough-and-tumble tactics. The team boasted

stars like Joe Medwick, Ripper Collins, Pepper Martin, and pitcher Dizzy Dean. The 1934 Cardinals won ninety-five games and beat the Detroit Tigers in seven games to win the World Series. Dean made more money barnstorming with Paige for a summer than he did all season playing for the Cardinals.

PAGE 33: *Jim Crow's Unwritten Laws*
Jim Crow laws throughout the South enforced racial segregation. Some of the laws, such as poll taxes and literacy tests to suppress minority voters, were written, and other laws were assumed. Decades of manners and customs, left over from the days of slavery, calcified into an etiquette, "humbling down": taking off your hat, using the back entrance of homes. This "etiquette" was demanded by whites, and to ignore it would mean risking your life. Blacks were often killed for just looking at a white woman or talking back to a white person.

PAGE 37: *Lynching*
In the last decades of the nineteenth century, the lynching of black people in the Southern and border states became a method used by whites to terrorize blacks. A uniquely American institution, lynching was the public murder of individuals suspected of "crimes," conceived and carried out by a mob. A lynching was a local community event. There were even postcards sold as mementos. Most often, lynchings were by hanging or shooting. Many were of a more heinous variety—burning at the stake, maiming, dismemberment, castration, and other forms of physical torture.

Southern politicians and officials often supported "lynch law," and came to power on a platform of white supremacy. State authorities often attempted to prevent lynchings, but seldom punished the mob participants. In *The Tragedy of Lynching* (1933), the sociologist Arthur F. Raper estimated, from his study of one hundred lynchings, that "at least one-half of the lynchings are carried out with police officers participating, and that in nine-tenths of the others the officers either condone or wink at the mob action."

PAGE 44: *The Role of Church*
Churches were a vital social institution and central to the African American community. Church revivals were great religious and social events. For sharecroppers, the church was the one place, besides the fields, they could congregate in large numbers. Gospels and hymns were sung with lyrics that praised the Lord, asked for the strength to persevere, and begged for deliverance and redemption.

Some churches became centers for political activity, leading the charge for improving housing, health care, and education. Like many of today's churches, they also provided charitable assistance, including food distribution and covering the costs of funerals. Relatives who lived elsewhere would send money to a church's minister to pass along instead of sending it directly to their family, fearing (with good reason) the property owner would take it.

The congregation depicted in this scene is from a Baptist church. Other denominations (such as the Methodists) performed their baptisms with a symbolic sprinkle of water. The Baptists, using John's baptism in the river Jordan as a model, favored full immersion.

PAGE 66: *Paige Has Arrived*
Paige rarely let a signed contract dictate where he should play, especially if a more lucrative offer was made. As a result, Paige routinely missed scheduled appearances. When he did arrive, he was often late. Paige may have walked slowly, but he drove fast, and being a passenger in his car meant risking your life. One time, already late to a game, Paige was pulled over for speeding. He was taken to a local judge and fined forty dollars. Paige handed the judge eighty dollars and said, "Here ya go, Mr. Judge, 'cause I'm coming back through tomorrow."

Page 74: The N-Word
"Out on the field, there'd be some white

folks in the stands," Satchel Paige said in his autobiography, *Maybe I'll Pitch Forever*. "Some of them'd call you [the N-word], but most would cheer you."

PAGE 75: *Calling in the Infielders*
Paige enhanced the intrinsic drama of baseball by injecting his own stunts. Calling in the fielders, a dramatic gesture, was a routine Paige performed many times. Paige's most legendary stunt occurred in the 1942 Negro World Series, when he was facing off against his onetime teammate Josh Gibson, the most feared black hitter of his day. With the game on the line, Paige walked two hitters to load the bases in order to pitch to Gibson. The crowd went wild as Paige then struck out Gibson with three pitches.

PAGE 80: *His Next Gig*
Paige went on to pitch for another thirty years! All told, his pitching career spanned six decades. In 1948, the year after Jackie Robinson broke into the big leagues, the 42-year-old Paige was signed by the Cleveland Indians and helped them win a World Series. In 1953, while Paige was playing for the St. Louis Browns, New York Yankees manager, Casey Stengel, selected Paige for the All-Star team. In 1965, the 59-year-old Satchel Paige, pitching for the Kansas City A's, threw three scoreless innings against the Boston Red Sox. Satchel Paige was inducted into the Baseball Hall of Fame on August 2, 1971. He continued to barnstorm, ending his career with the Tulsa Oilers in 1976. Paige died in Kansas City in 1982.

Bibliography

Chafe, William Henry, Gavins, Raymond, and Korstad, Robert. *Remembering Jim Crow: African Americans Tell About Life in the Segregated South*. The New Press, New York, 2001.

Paige, Satchel and Lipman, David. *Maybe I'll Pitch Forever: A Great Baseball Player Tells the Hilarious Story Behind the Legend*. University of Nebraska Press, 1993.

Ribowsky, Mark. *Don't Look Back: Satchel Paige in the Shadows of Baseball*. Da Capo Press, New York, 1994.

Rosengarten, Theodore. *All God's Dangers: The Life of Nate Shaw*. Alfred A. Knopf, New York, 1975.

Credits

WRITER AND SERIES EDITOR
JAMES STURM is a cartoonist and the cofounder of the Center for Cartoon Studies. His graphic novels include *The Golem's Mighty Swing*, *Market Day*, and *Off Season*. His picture books for children include *Ape and Armadillo Take Over the World*, *Birdsong*, and the Adventures in Cartooning series (with Andrew Arnold and Alexis Frederick-Frost).

ARTIST
RICH TOMMASO is mostly known for his series of crime novels, which include *Clover Honey*, *Sam Hill: The Cavalier Mr. Thompson*, *Dark Corridor*, and *Dry County*. He is currently drawing a new Dick Tracy comic series with Mike Lee and Laura Allred, and he has also made a dozen other comics and graphic novels in various genres, including *Spy Seal*, *She Wolf*, *Vikings' End*, *Don't Look Back*, *8 ½ Ghosts*, *Perverso!*, *The Horror of Collier County*, and *Let's Hit the Road*. Rich lives in Atlanta, Georgia, with his girlfriend, Amy, and their two cats.

INTRODUCTION
GERALD EARLY is a noted essayist and American culture critic and director of the Center for the Humanities at Washington University in St. Louis. Early is the author of several books, including *The Culture of Bruising: Essays on Prizefighting, Literature, and Modern American Culture*, which won the 1994 National Book Critics Circle Award for criticism. He is also the editor of numerous volumes, including *Body Language: Writers on Sport* (1998), *The Muhammad Ali Reader* (1998), *The Sammy Davis, Jr. Reader* (2001), and *Miles Davis and American Culture* (2001). He served as a consultant on Ken Burns's documentary films on baseball and jazz, both of which aired on PBS.

Illustration this page: Kevin Huizenga

THE CENTER FOR CARTOON STUDIES produces comics, zines, posters, and graphic novels (like this book about Satchel Paige!). For those interested in making comics themselves one day, the Center for Cartoon Studies is also America's finest cartooning school—offering one- and two-year courses of study, master of fine arts degrees, and summer workshops.